Contents

Published in this edition by Galley Press, an imprint of
W.H. Smith and Son Limited. Registered No. 237811 England.
Trading as WHS Distributors, St John's House, East Street, Leicester, LE1 6NE.
Copyright © Art Work and text produced by Martspress Limited. 23 Nork Way,
Banstead, Surrey, SM7 1PB. 1985
in association with Patrick Hawkey & Co. Ltd.

ISBN 0 86136 787 1

Printed and bound by Brepols N.V. – Turnhout, Belgium

The Tinder Box
and other stories

Stories adapted by Barbara Hayes
Illustrated by Ronald and Gerry Embleton

The Tinder Box

Many years ago, in a far country, a young soldier came striding back from the wars.

Left! Right! Left! Right! His feet struck the ground boldly as he marched along the highway, with his knapsack on his back and his sword at his side.

Along the dusty way, he met an old lady. The soldier did not know it, but the woman was a witch. The soldier smiled at her.

She pointed her finger at him so the soldier halted and saluted her.

"Good evening, my good man," cackled the witch. "What a fine upstanding fellow you are! How proud you look in your splendid uniform with your trusty sword ready to protect you. A young man like you must need a lot of money for your adventures. I'm sure that if you happened to find some, you would spend it well."

"Good evening to you," replied the soldier. "And thank you for your kind words. But what is all this talk of money?"

"You will have all the money you can carry, if you will only do me a favour," replied the ugly, old witch.

She pointed to a big tree. "That tree is hollow inside," she said. "Climb to the top and you will see a hole into which you can let yourself down. Right down under the tree you will have to go, but do not fear. I will tie a rope round your waist and will haul you up again when you call."

"What do you want me to do under the tree?" asked the soldier.

"Fill your pockets with money," grinned the ugly, old witch. "When you get to the bottom of the tree, you will find yourself in a wide passage. It will be very bright. The passage is lit by a hundred blazing lamps. In front of you will be three doors.

"They are locked, but you will be able to open them. The keys are there. If you go into the first room, you will see a box in the middle of the floor. A dog is guarding it and he has eyes as big as saucers. Do not worry about that, I will give you my blue-checked apron, which you can spread out on the floor.

"Go forward swiftly and slip the apron under the dog. It will not harm you. Then open the box and take out as much money as you like. In this room it will all be copper, but if you would rather have silver, go into the next room.

"There you will find a dog with eyes as big as millstones. Do not be concerned. Slip my apron under him and take as much silver as you can carry. However, if you prefer, go into the third room. There is plenty of gold there. In the third room, you will find a dog with eyes as big as round towers.

"Do not let that concern you, even though he is the largest dog you will ever have seen. Slip my apron under him and he will not harm you. Open the box he is guarding and take out as much gold from it as you can possibly carry." The soldier was wary.

"That sounds all very well for me," he said, "but what do you want, old lady? You must want something, even if you don't want money."

"You are right. I don't want one penny," replied the ugly, old woman. "I only want you to bring me back the old tinder box my grandmother forgot to bring up."

"Very well. Tie the rope around my waist," agreed the soldier. The witch did so, then took off her blue-checked apron and handed it to the gallant young soldier. They walked over to the hole in the tree. Then the soldier scrambled into the trunk and let himself down into the darkness.

Down, down the soldier went, until his eyes were suddenly dazzled by light. As the old woman had said, he found himself in a wide passageway lit by a hundred blazing lamps.

In front of him were three doors. He unlocked the first and stepped into a room.

Brave soldier though he was, he gasped with dismay at what he saw in front of him. Guarding a large box was a dog with eyes as big as saucers.

The dog's burning eyes stared at him.

"Good dog! Nice boy!" gasped the soldier and hurrying forward, he slipped the witch's apron under one of the paws of the terrifying dog. Sure enough, the dog took no further notice of him. The soldier filled his pockets and his knapsack with copper coins, thinking what a fortunate fellow he was. Then he shut the box, took up the blue-checked apron and hurried into the next room. What a fearful sight awaited the soldier! In that room sat a dog with eyes as big as millstones, and which blazed at him fiercely. The soldier trembled.

"Good boy! Nice dog!" gulped the young man as he hurried forward and pushed the witch's apron under one of the dog's massive paws. The soldier was delighted to find himself ignored, and turning out the copper coins from his pockets and knapsack, he refilled them with silver.

"I am now a rich man!" the soldier smiled to himself. "I shall be able to eat the very finest food . . . I shall live in the most elegant rooms . . . I shall wear wonderful clothes, too! With all this money I can buy a fine horse and never have to trudge on foot ever again!" But then the soldier began to wonder about the next room with the

dog with eyes as big as round towers. He sounded even more fearsome than the other creatures he had already met – but in that room were coins of *gold!*

"I will never have a chance like this again," thought the soldier. "And since I am here, surely I should dare to enter the third room and fill my pockets and knapsack with *gold*. Silver is fine enough, but gold must be better. With a fortune in gold I could live magnificently for the rest of my life. I need never be cold again – nor even chilly! I could marry a pretty wife and live happily ever after!"

But then he wondered about the third dog. Did he really need to face such a beast?

The soldier's greed overcame his fear.

"I *will* try to get the gold," he thought. "In any case, I must go on. I have not found that tinder box yet."

He snatched up the old witch's blue-checked apron and hurried out of the second room. He turned the key in the lock of the third room and pushed open the door.

He was at the head of a long, steep staircase leading down into a cavern-like room. In the room sat the most terrifying creature the soldier had ever seen.

It was an enormous dog with eyes as big as round towers. The eyes rolled round and round like wheels. Then they turned and came to rest on the soldier and stared at him with a burning light.

"Good evening," the soldier said politely to the huge dog with the eyes as big as round towers.

He gave a smart salute. A dog like this must be treated with great respect.

The dog said nothing. It did nothing.

At last the soldier thought: "Well, I will try doing the same as I did with the other dogs. I just hope it works!"

He hurried forward and slipped the old witch's blue-checked apron under a heavy paw. The soldier was relieved when the dog took no further notice of him. The young man threw open a chest and found that it was indeed filled with gold. He was overjoyed. He turned the silver out of his pockets and his knapsack and refilled them with gold coins.

Then, lying on a stone near the chest of gold, the soldier saw a tinder box.

"That must be the box the old woman wanted," he thought. "I mustn't forget I said that I would take it to her."

He picked up the tinder box and put it in his pocket.

Staggering under the weight of the heavy gold, the soldier then clambered back towards the wide hallway where the hundred lamps were still blazing.

The soldier walked past the doorway of the room with the dog with eyes like millstones. He walked past the door of the room where he had seen the dog with eyes as big as saucers.

He shivered at the thought of the dangers he had somehow managed to overcome.

He walked to the foot of the long slope which led out into the sweet, fresh air. He was longing for the sunshine.

He retied the rope round his waist and called up to the old woman, who was waiting at the top.

"Haul me up now, old lady," he shouted.

"Do you have the tinder box?" the witch called down.

"Yes. To be sure, I have it," the soldier shouted back.

So the witch hauled the soldier back up through the dark and damp, narrow hole under the tree.

The soldier scrambled through the hole and joined the old lady who was holding out her gnarled hand.

"Give me the tinder box," she demanded.

The soldier was puzzled. He could not understand why the old woman wanted none of the gold, but only a scruffy, old tinder box. He was intrigued.

"Why do you want it?" he asked.

"Mind your own business!" snapped the witch. "*You* have your money, as promised. Give *me* the tinder box."

Now the soldier was newly come from the wars. He was used to fighting first and arguing later.

"Tell me why you want the tinder box or I shall draw my sword and cut off your head!" he shouted. The witch was furious.

"I am a witch. I don't have to tell you!" screamed the old woman, who always expected people to be afraid of her.

The soldier drew his sword and with one stroke, he put an end to the old witch *and* the argument!

Then, with the tinder box in his pocket and laden with gold, the soldier marched into the nearest town.

He walked straight to the grandest hotel, rented the most expensive rooms and sent for all the food he liked best.

"I am a rich man. I shall have what I like and do what I like," he thought.

The hotel servants who came to clean his boots thought they were shabby old things for so rich a gentleman but the next day the soldier bought new boots, and elegant clothes.

After that, everyone believed he was, and always had been, a rich man.

He led a merry life. He went to the theatre and concerts. He drove everywhere in a fine carriage. He had lots of friends who were always flocking to dinner with him and telling him what a fine fellow he was. His company was sought after.

The soldier loved that.

These new friends laughed at all his jokes and said what a witty fellow he was. The soldier loved that too and invited them to dinner again. How he enjoyed himself!

His friends wondered if the fun could last. It did for many long, merry months, but eventually the end came. The day dawned when the soldier had spent all his money except for a few coins he had received in change from his last gold piece.

He had to move out of his expensive apartment. Now all he could afford was a cheap, comfortless room high up in the attic. He had to sell all the elegant clothes and rich ornaments and jewellery he had bought for himself in the good days.

He hoped that some of his nice, new friends would ask him back to dinner in return for the many dinners he had lavished upon them so generously.

However, his so-called "friends" did not.

They did not even climb up to visit him in his new, shabby room. There was some talk about the stairs being too steep and too many for them.

When they saw the soldier in the street, they did not seem to recognize him, and passed by without speaking.

If he spoke to them, they did not answer him. They hurried along as if he were invisible.

It was all very upsetting.

One evening, the soldier sat in his shabby, cold, unlit room with not a penny to his name.

Suddenly he remembered the tinder box.

"There was a small piece of candle in that box," he thought. "At least I can have some light in this dingy room."

He took the tinder box from his old jacket pocket and struck once to make a spark.

As the spark flew from the flint, the door of the room burst open and in raced the dog with the eyes as big as saucers!

It was the dog he had last seen in the room opening from the first passageway with the hundred blazing lights.

The dog with eyes as big as saucers stood before the astonished young soldier.

It said: "What does my lord command?"

The soldier was delighted to be asked such a question. "What a marvellous tinder box this is," he gasped. "No wonder that old witch wanted to keep it."

He looked at the dog with eyes as big as saucers. "I command that you fetch me a bag of money."

The dog raced out of the room and in what seemed like no time at all, he returned with a bag of copper coins.

The soldier was happy and relieved to see the bag of copper coins. Now he was no longer poor. However, he could not help thinking about the other dogs and the treasures of silver and gold which they had guarded.

He turned back to the tinder box. He picked up the flint and struck twice. At once the dog with eyes as big as millstones ran into the room.

"Fetch me some money," ordered the soldier.

In a moment the dog was back with a bag of *silver* coins.

The soldier could have wept for joy. With trembling hands he struck the flint three times. As he hoped, the dog with eyes as big as round towers rushed into the room.

"What does my lord command?" asked the huge dog.

"Fetch me some money," ordered the soldier, who was feeling much better.

The dog was gone for only a few seconds and then it returned with a bag of gold.

The soldier was beside himself with delight. He moved into comfortable rooms once more, bought back his nice clothes and started eating well again.

Then one day he heard talk of a mysterious princess. She was the daughter of the king and very beautiful. However, there had been a prophesy that she would one day meet and marry a common soldier.

Such an idea filled the king with horror.

He kept his daughter shut away in a strong castle and no one but her family and her maid were allowed to see her.

One evening when the soldier was in his room with the dog with eyes as big as saucers, he said, "I do wish I could see that mysterious princess who is kept locked away, even if only for a moment."

At once the dog rushed out of the room. It went to the bedroom of the princess, lifted her on to its back and took her, still sleeping, to show its master.

The soldier fell in love with the princess at once and kissed her, but then the dog took her back to her own room.

In the morning the princess sat eating breakfast with the king and queen.

"I had the most curious dream last night," said the princess. "I dreamed that a huge dog with eyes as big as saucers came to my room. It lifted me on to its back and carried me through the streets to the room of a soldier who kissed me. Then the dog brought me home."

The king and queen were not pleased, especially at the mention of a soldier.

"We don't want that prophesy about our daughter marrying a common soldier to be fulfilled," said the king.

They instructed the princess's maid to keep watch over her throughout the night.

"If the princess is only dreaming, then there is no harm done," said the queen. "But if you see this terrible dog, then strange powers are most certainly at work and we must beware."

Night came. The princess went to sleep. The maid sat up on watch, hoping that nothing would disturb the peace of the night.

Before long there was a padding and scratching of feet. A mighty dog came running into the room. It picked up the princess and carried her away.

The clever dog took some chalk in its mouth and marked all the doors for streets around with a cross.

The next morning the princess sat at breakfast with the king and queen.

"I had that strange dream again last night," she said, "the one about the dog and the soldier."

At once the king and queen sent for the maid. She told them that it was no dream, but that it had happened.

"I will take you to the house where the soldier lives," said the maid.

However, when she reached the right street, she could not pick out the house.

The maid was a brave and faithful girl. She jumped into her boots and raced through the streets after the dog and the princess. She saw them go through the door of a big house.

Even this good maid did not dare to go into the house, but she marked the door with a cross, so that she would know it again. Then she went back to the castle and presently the dog brought the sleeping princess back to her own bed.

On the way back to its master, the dog noticed the cross on the door.

"Someone followed me," it thought. "No one must know where I take the princess or there will be trouble for my master."

Crosses were on many of the the doors and the girl could not recall which house it had been.

The king and queen, who had brought along their guards to arrest this upstart soldier, were disappointed, but the queen was not unduly dismayed.

The queen was much more than a pretty face. She was a clever woman. She took her big gold scissors and cut up a large piece of silk into small sections which she made into a pretty little bag. This she filled with grains of wheat and tied it to the back of the princess's nightdress. Then she cut a little hole in the bag, so that the grains would gradually drop out, leaving a trail wherever the princess went.

At night the dog came again, took the princess on its back and ran off with her to the soldier, who by this time was so in love with her that he longed to be a prince, in order that he might reasonably ask for permission to have the princess as his wife.

The dog did not notice the grain as it dropped out all along the road from the castle to the soldier's door. However, the king's guards noticed it. They followed the dog and the princess and made note of the house to which they were led.

In the morning, the king and queen ordered the soldier to be seized and thrown into a dungeon.

The poor soldier was most upset. The dungeon was dark and depressing. He had left the tinder box behind in his rooms and was powerless to help himself.

Then one day the guards told him he was to be hanged next morning. The soldier stared hopelessly from the barred window of his cell. How could he possibly escape?

He saw a young boy hurrying along and called to him: "If you will run an errand for me, I will give you a silver coin," said the soldier.

At once the boy came close to listen.

"I left a tinder box in my room. Please fetch it for me," said the soldier. He also told the boy how to get into his room.

Fortunately the boy was both honest and a swift runner. He fetched the tinder box and handed it to the soldier as he stood on the scaffold. He had been thinking that his last hour on this earth had finally come.

The soldier looked across at the king.

"Will you grant me one last request?" he asked.

"Yes. If it is nothing much," snapped the king. "What *is* your last request?"

"Let me strike the flint from my old tinder box and get a light to smoke a last pipe," begged the soldier.

"Hurry up about it then," called back the king, little realizing to what he was agreeing.

The soldier struck the flint once and the dog with eyes as big as saucers appeared

and bounded towards the scaffold.

The soldier then struck the flint twice and the dog with eyes as big as millstones appeared.

The soldier struck the flint three times and the dog with eyes as big as round towers appeared.

There was a strange silence, as everyone stared at the enormous dogs.

"Release me and let me marry the princess," the soldier called to the king.

"Never!" shouted the king. "Impossible!"

Then one of the dogs seized the king and shook him as he would have shaken a rat.

"On the other hand," gasped the poor king, "perhaps you are not such a *common* soldier after all. In fact, you are quite an *unusual* soldier. You may marry the princess."

The soldier gave a big sigh of relief and happiness. He remembered to give the silver coin to the little boy and the preparations for the wedding were made.

It took place at the palace and the dogs sat at the wedding feast and stared at everyone with their big, round eyes.

The Knight and the Dragon

In the far west of the Pacific Ocean lie several islands, which make up the land of Japan.

Many, many years ago a huge and fierce dragon was tormenting the people of one of these islands.

The dragon was bigger than a house. It was almost bigger than a palace. It was a horrible mauve-pink colour. One of its feet was as big as a man. Each scaly toe ended in an enormous, curved talon as sharp as a dagger.

Its lashing tail was long and pointed and worst of all, the dragon breathed *fire!*

The enormous dragon roamed freely all over the countryside, scorching the farmers' crops growing in the fields, with its fiery breath.

It munched the apples from the trees in the orchards. It ate the animals from the farms. It roared and waved its huge tail and trampled with its huge feet. It was a trial and a trouble to everyone.

"We really must do something about getting rid of that pest," said the king.

Many brave warriors went to try to slay the dragon, but he was too big and fierce for all of them.

Now even the fiercest dragon in the world can only be in one place at a time and this was quite a big island. While the dragon was eating and rampaging in one part of the island, in another part, life could be peaceful for months on end.

Sometimes, after the dragon had swallowed a plump sheep and then crunched his way through a sack or two of carrots, which he considered were good for his skin, he would find a quiet place and go to sleep for several weeks at a time.

Then everything would be pleasant again and it was possible to forget the dragon – until the next time it appeared.

It was especially easy to forget the bothersome dragon if you had something else on your mind, like being in love, as the king's lovely daughter and the brave, young Shikoka were.

Shikoka was young and handsome and from a good family. He had been trained as a warrior and he was a very suitable young man to marry the princess.

They were both so happy, thinking they had no problems and that the king would allow them to marry as soon as they asked his permission.

However, when Shikoka finally did bow low before the king and ask if he could marry the princess, he received an extremely unpleasant surprise.

"I don't see how I can let you marry the princess when there are so many brave men going off to fight the dragon and coming back wounded from their courageous attempts," said the king. "I really should say that the princess may only marry the man who rids our island of the torment of this greedy dragon."

Shikoka blinked and dragged his thoughts away from his beloved princess. "Dragon? What dragon?" he asked.

"Dear me. You have been living in a dream world for the last few months,"

sighed the king. "A huge, fierce dragon is rampaging through the island, burning and destroying. Unless you can rid us of it, you may not marry the princess."

"If a job needs to be done, it should be done immediately," said Shikoka. He said goodbye to the princess, sharpened his sword, burnished his spear, saw that his horse was in fine form and rode out to fight the dragon.

On the way he saw a merchant who was sneezing and *sneezing*. "I am selling something new called pepper," explained the merchant. "It makes food taste good, but my word, it does make one sneeze. I just simply cannot stop sneezing!"

Shikoka bought the merchant's whole supply of pepper and rode on to find the dragon. He did this with no difficulty at all. He rode round a rock and there was the dragon lying in wait.

"BEEEEGONE!" hissed the dragon, breathing fire and flame. Shikoka's horse was terrified. It reared up and Shikoka was thrown from the saddle.

The young knight hit the rough, stony ground with a painful crash. However, he was a brave and clever man. He had been told that bigger, more experienced warriors than he, had been unable to defeat the dragon by fighting. Shikoka knew he must drive the dragon from the land by cunning, not brute force.

Keeping his wits about him, the young knight rolled round to face his fearsome enemy. The heat of the flames scorched his face. The smell of the dragon's scaly body choked him.

"It's now or never!" thought Shikoka.

He loosened the wrappings on the pepper and threw it into the face of the dragon.

The dragon was drawing in a mighty breath, ready to shoot out fire at the small figure of Shikoka. The pepper went in with the air and soon the dragon was coughing and sneezing helplessly.

Shikoka rolled out of reach and picked up his weapons. He did not need them.

"I have had enough of this place," choked the dragon. He swam away out to sea and never came back again.

Shikoka was delighted. On his way to the palace, he told the merchant to keep him well supplied with pepper in case another dragon should ever decide to visit the island.

Then Shikoka married his princess and they lived happily ever after. Everyone on the island was so pleased the dragon was gone, they gave Shikoka and the princess many beautiful wedding presents.

The Beggar Princess

Long ago and far away, there lived two rich sisters. Their father had been a clever merchant. Now, unfortunately, he was dead.

However, he had left plenty of money to be shared equally between the two girls.

One of the girls, named Anna, was very kind-hearted. Whenever she saw a beggar or someone who looked the least bit worse off that herself, she dropped coins into their hands. The other sister did not approve of this kind of open-handedness at all.

"You will soon run through your money if you carry on like that!" said Griselda, the other sister. "Money does not grow on trees, you know."

"Oh, but it makes the poor people so happy, if I help them," replied Anna. "Look how they smile when they see me!"

"Of course they smile when they see you!" snapped Griselda. "They see you coming from the other side of town, you complete simpleton. Every lazybones in the district comes and smiles at you to get

some of your money. And they're never disappointed!"

Anna took no notice of the hard words of her sister and continued giving money and food to the poor.

Of course the day did come when Anna ran out of money.

"I am sure you will let me go on living and eating with you, dear sister," she said, knowing that she would have been kind to her sister, if Griselda had been poor. But Anna had a rude awakening.

"No. I will certainly *not* let you live with me," snapped Griselda. "Father left you as much money as he left to me. If you have spent all yours, that is your bad management. I don't see why I should suffer for it."

"But I did not *waste* my money," gasped Anna. "I gave it to help poor people who were in need. Surely you will now help me, your only sister. It is not as if I spent my money on having a good time or on a lot of expensive clothes."

"More fool you, then," replied Griselda. "You did not even enjoy your money for the little time that you had it. But that is nothing to do with me. As far as I am concerned, you are a useless mouth to feed. Now begone with you. Go to the beggars and see if they have any of your money left. Perhaps they will give some of it back to you! Ha! Ha!"

With those taunts Anna was turned out, penniless, into the snow.

As it happened, Anna did go to live with the beggars. She had no other choice. Fortunately, they did remember her and her kindness. They welcomed her and shared with her what little they had.

Times were hard in the winter, but spring came at last. The weather became warmer and the first flowers bloomed. The beggars made a crown of blossoms and put them on Anna's head.

"You were like a princess to us once," they said. "Perhaps you will bring us good luck again sometime."

Good luck was closer than any of them realized.

A prince from the next kingdom was looking for a wife. With his followers, he came to town and it was arranged that all the rich young ladies should go to a party to meet him.

The prince's father had told him he must be sure to marry a wealthy girl because that was the correct thing for a prince to do.

However, this young prince was rather like Anna. He did not always do the wise thing. He frequently allowed his heart to rule his head.

On the way into town the prince's party

passed the beggars' camp. They saw Anna, who was so healthy and beautiful, it was obvious she could not have been a beggar for long. He made some discreet inquiries about her.

When the prince learned who she was and what she had done, he fell in love with her at once. "She is a girl after my own heart," he said. He asked Anna to marry him and Anna accepted joyfully.

The prince had found a wife, but he did not cancel the big party arranged in town. He turned it into a wedding party and invited the beggars as well as the rich townsfolk.

Griselda felt annoyed that her penniless sister had the prince as her husband. It did not seem fair nor just.

But amongst the prince's attendants was a courtier called Stingy Grabalot. He was looking for a wife who would help him to get together a roomful of gold to keep them happy in their old age. He was quite determined to marry a careful woman.

Of course, Griselda was *just* the wife for him. They married and lived richly ever after, so in the end both sisters were happy in their own way.

The Flying Horse

Long ago, in the land of Persia, there lived a prince who had the most amazing adventures upon the back of a wonderful enchanted horse.

It all started on the day of the festival of Nooroze, when the prince's father, the elderly sultan, was holding court in his magnificent palace. Many folk were there.

A Hindu came and stood at the foot of the sultan's throne. With him he had the most astonishing artificial horse. It was richly bridled and saddled and so skilfully made that at first glance it seemed to be real. Everyone was most intrigued by it.

The Hindu bowed before the sultan and pointed to the horse.

"This animal is a great wonder," he said. "I have only to sit on its back and I can be transported to any part of the world, in a very short time. Then the horse will bring me safely back again."

"This is a wondrous thing, which you

greatly liked to collect the unusual and the curious.

"Tell me your price for this wonderful horse," he said. "I truly desire to own it."

"Sire," replied the Hindu, "I will only part with my horse on one condition – that you give me the hand of your daughter in marriage."

A gasp ran round the court. A mere merchant was not fit even to *think* of marrying the sultan's daughter.

Standing amongst the courtiers was Prince Feroze, the eldest son of the sultan and his heir. Knowing how his father loved curious things, the prince was filled with fear that the sultan might agree to the Hindu's request.

"Such a marriage would bring shame upon the family," thought the prince. "I must act to stop it."

Stepping forward, the prince said: "Father, allow me to sit on the horse's back and try its worth. Perhaps I can then suggest the true price which you should pay for such a curiosity."

The Hindu eagerly agreed to this, as in truth he was only seeking to make a good bargain with the sultan.

claim," replied the sultan. "Prove it to me, or I shall remain never believing you."

The sultan pointed to a far mountain. "Ride your horse to a hill at the foot of that mountain," he said. "Bring me back a branch from a palm which grows in that place only. Then I will believe that your horse can do as you claim."

At once the Hindu put his foot into the stirrup and mounted the horse. He turned a peg which was in a hollow of the horse's back near the saddle. Immediately, the horse rose into the air amidst the gasps of the amazed courtiers. With the speed of the wind it flew towards the distant mountain and was soon out of sight.

In a quarter of an hour the Hindu and the horse returned. Twice they circled the walls of the palace while all the townsfolk looked up at them in wonder.

Then the horse came back to land on the spot from which it had flown. The Hindu dismounted, went to kneel before the sultan and presented him with the palm branch for which he had asked.

At once the sultan was filled with desire to own the horse. He was a man who

The sultan nodded his agreement and Prince Feroze put his foot into the stirrup and leaped on to the decorated saddle of the wonderful horse.

The Hindu stepped forward to instruct the prince on how to manage the horse, for as well as the peg near the saddle, there was another peg which had to be turned in order to bring the rider home again.

However, Prince Feroze was too proud to take instructions from a merchant. Besides that, he wished to prove to his father that the horse could easily be managed and was no great thing that needed to be purchased at the high price of an unworthy marriage.

As he had seen the Hindu work it, Prince Feroze turned the peg in the horse's back. At once he rose into the air with great speed. In a few seconds he was beyond earshot. In a few minutes he was out of sight over the horizon.

The Hindu was in despair. He knew that without proper instructions the prince might never be able to bring the horse back to Persia.

When the minutes and the hours went by and the prince did not return, the sultan became wracked with worry and consumed with grief. He threw the Hindu into prison and said he would stay there until the prince returned safely.

Meanwhile, Prince Feroze had soared higher and higher into the air. At first he enjoyed the wonderful view of the trees and mountains and rivers and houses. Then, as the horse continued to climb ever higher, the prince became alarmed. He pulled and twisted at the peg near the saddle but he continued to fly higher.

In desperation the prince felt all over the horse's back and neck. At last his groping fingers chanced upon the other smaller peg behind the horse's right ear. With trembling hands he turned it and to his immense relief, he felt the horse begin to make a slow descent.

By now Prince Feroze was hundreds of miles from his home and darkness had fallen. He felt the horse's hooves touch ground. Dismounting, he could dimly see that he was on the roof of a large building. He crept downstairs and peeped through a window. His gaze fell upon a beautiful girl.

The size of the rooms and the beautiful furnishings left Prince Feroze in no doubt that he had landed on a palace.

From the elegance of her clothes, he guessed that the sleeping girl must be a princess.

The prince was in a dangerous position. He could be taken for a thief and punished. Even if the people in the palace believed he was an honest man, he might still be treated badly and made to work as a servant for the rest of his life. Yet he needed help. He was cold and tired and hungry after his long flight. He needed food and rest before he could attempt to fly back to his home.

The prince looked again at the sleeping girl. She had a kind face. He decided to throw himself on her mercy.

He walked slowly forward and tried to awaken the girl without startling her. As he tugged gently at her sleeve, she

flickered her eyes open and stared at him in disbelief.

How could a stranger have reached her without waking the guards?

Quickly the prince told his story of the enchanted horse and his long and dangerous flight.

"Have no fear," smiled the girl. "You have landed in Bengal where we treat strangers with respect and courtesy. I am the Princess of Bengal and this is the palace built for me by my father – away from the noise and dirt of the city."

"I will call my servants to wait on you," continued the princess. "You must rest after the dangers you have been through."

She awoke her servants. They were amazed to see a strange young man in the palace but none of the servants would disobey the princess. They led Prince Feroze to a beautiful suite of rooms. They showed him to a room where he could bathe and they put out clean clothes for him. They prepared a light meal to refresh the young man. He slept restfully on smooth silken sheets until morning.

The Princess of Bengal thought Prince Feroze the most handsome and charming man she had ever seen.

Next morning she took great care to dress in her most becoming clothes and to put on her finest jewellery. She was in love.

"Tell the Prince of Persia he may come to see me now," she told her servants.

They fetched Prince Feroze, who bowed low and thanked the princess for all her kindess.

"Now may I have your permission to leave for my home?" he asked. "My father will be concerned at my absence."

"It is not right that you should go so soon," said the Princess of Bengal. "It is not often that we have a visitor from so far away as Persia. Tell us what your country is like. What do you eat? What are your customs? We like to learn all we can of distant countries."

Prince Feroze felt it would be churlish not to do as the princess asked. He sat and told her about Persia. Every day she made another excuse to keep him in Bengal. She

charmed him with picnics by the river, with singing and with displays of dancing.

For two months Prince Feroze stayed in Bengal and became deeply in love with the princess.

However, at last he knew he must go home. Declaring his love for the princess, he asked her to go with him, for he could not endure the thought of life without her.

"There is nothing my heart desires more," whispered the princess. "My only fear is of that horse. Will it carry us safely to Persia or run wild for hundreds of miles?"

The Prince assured the Princess of Bengal that now he had discovered the way to control the enchanted horse, their journey to Persia would be swift and safe.

The beautiful girl bade goodbye to her family and, sitting behind the prince on the back of the enchanted horse, prepared to fly away to a new life in a far country.

Prince Feroze turned the peg near the horse's saddle and they flew upwards.

Now skilled in controlling the horse, Prince Feroze flew back to Persia in two hours. He landed at his summer palace outside the city, where the servants greeted him with joy.

He ordered them to prepare a fine apartment for the Princess of Bengal. He then intended to leave the girl in the palace while he rode to the city to ask his father's consent to their marriage.

"You are a great princess," he explained, "and my father will want to greet you with due ceremony and splendour as befits the honour of our country."

The sultan wept with joy when he saw his eldest son home safely, for all hope of his return had recently been abandoned.

Prince Feroze quickly described his amazing adventures and explained that the Princess of Bengal was waiting out at his summer palace.

The Sultan was so overwhelmed with joy, he scarcely knew what he was doing, but he did remember the Hindu from whom he had sought the horse and who was still lying in prison.

He had him brought before him. "As you see, the prince is safely returned," said the sultan to the Hindu. "For that reason I will spare your life. But take your horse and go. I never want to see you here again."

With that, the Hindu was thrown out of the palace.

The Hindu ran through the courtyards

to find his enchanted horse. He was angry and resentful. For weeks he had lain in a dirty prison and all because the prince had taken his horse without bothering to find out how to use it. The Hindu felt he had done no wrong and had been badly treated. He was determined to get his revenge.

He learned from his guards that the prince hoped to marry the Princess of Bengal, who was at the summer palace.

Hurrying there on the enchanted horse, the Hindu sought out and spoke to the captain of the guard.

"I have been sent to carry the Princess of Bengal to the city on this enchanted horse," he said. "Please bring her to me at once."

The captain of the guard was doubtful for a moment, but it seemed quite fitting for a princess to travel on an enchanted horse, so he agreed.

The Princess of Bengal herself was quite happy to go with the Hindu. She recognized the horse and did not doubt that her beloved, Prince Feroze, had sent it.

With no thought of danger, the princess mounted the horse behind the Hindu and allowed herself to be taken away.

Meanwhile the sultan and all his court, dressed in their finest robes, were advancing along the road from the city towards the summer palace.

Prince Feroze, also dressed in his greatest finery, was riding ahead of them to alert the princess that his father was approaching.

How horrified they were, when looking into the sky above their heads, they saw the Hindu riding away on the enchanted horse, with the Princess of Bengal sitting behind him.

The princess was still not alarmed. She thought the Hindu was doing as he had promised and was taking her to her prince.

However, when he swooped over the finely-dressed courtiers and laughed and jeered and called to them that he had tricked them, that *he* had the Princess of Bengal and that *they* would never see her again, she became terrified.

She screamed and shouted for help, but she dared not jump from the horse because she was so high above the ground.

The prince and the sultan and the throng of courtiers all shouted back. They waved their fists and called out that they had never before encountered such treachery and insolence.

The Hindu laughed in response and turning, flew far away with the princess. There was nothing anyone could do to stop him. A sadness descended over Persia.

On the swift back of the enchanted horse, the Hindu and the Princess of Bengal were soon hundreds of miles away above the land of the Sultan of Kashmir.

Choosing a lonely forest spot, the Hindu landed and turned to the princess.

"Hidden nearby is my home where I made the enchanted horse," he said. "You will live here with me and be my wife."

"I will *never* be your wife," replied the princess. "You are unworthy to be the husband of the Princess of Bengal."

At that, the Hindu started to beat the princess, screaming at her that she would soon learn to do as she was told and that she was no fine princess here in the depths of the forest.

As luck would have it, all the shouting and screeching did not go unheard even in that lonely woodland. The Sultan of Kashmir was returning from a hunting trip and dismounted to see what was causing the commotion.

"I am beating my insolent wife. There is no need for you to interfere," the Hindu said to the sultan.

Now that is no way to speak to a sultan and in addition the sultan could see that the Princess of Bengal did not in any way look like the wife of a merchant.

"Tell me *your* story," he said to the princess and this she did as quickly as she could draw breath.

At once the proud sultan flew into a rage.

The impertinent Hindu must be punished.

"Off with his head!" he cried, pointing at the Hindu. Then he smiled at the Princess of Bengal. "Come to my palace where I will give you shelter," he said.

The princess was overjoyed, and thought that after a rest she would be allowed to go back to her beloved Prince of Persia. Such happiness was not to be.

"I will do you the honour of marrying you myself," announced the sultan, to the horror of the princess.

The unfortunate girl was in the power of the sultan and she dared not make a direct refusal. Instead, she pretended to be mad and went into screaming fits if the word marriage was so much as mentioned.

Meanwhile, the heartbroken Prince of Persia was seeking his lost beloved. Without the enchanted horse, he could travel only slowly. However, Prince Feroze was so much in love with the Princess of Bengal, he would have travelled all his life in order to find her.

After many months of journeying, the sad young man came to Kashmir. Here he heard talk of a Princess of Bengal who was living at the palace of the sultan and who had gone mad.

"The sultan has sent for many doctors, but the princess screams at the sight of them," said the gossips. "The sultan is at his wits end to know how to cure her."

At once, Prince Feroze hurried to the palace. He sent a message through the palace guards to say that although he was young, he was a skilled physician and he was sure he could cure the princess.

The sultan saw him at once. "The Princess of Bengal screams at the sight of all physicians," sighed the sultan.

"She will not scream at the sight of me,"

smiled Prince Feroze, feeling confident.

To the amazement of the courtiers, the princess did not scream when the new, young physician walked into the room.

"You have worked a miracle already," smiled the Sultan of Kashmir. "Can you

possibly make the princess well enough to marry me?"

"I must speak to her alone," replied Prince Feroze. "It is the only way."

At once the sultan ordered everyone to withdraw and leave the new physician alone with the princess.

At last the delighted prince and princess were able to tell each other of their adventures.

"But what happened to the enchanted horse?" asked Prince Feroze. "With it we could escape so easily."

"The sultan has locked it in his treasure house," whispered the princess. "He knows it is precious, but he does not know how to use it."

"Be prepared to leave on the horse tomorrow," ordered the prince. Then he went back to speak to the sultan.

"I understand everything that is wrong with the princess," said Prince Feroze, which indeed he did. "I can make her well quite easily."

The Sultan of Kashmir was delighted. "Tell me what to do," he begged.

"Tomorrow, bring the enchanted horse on which the princess arrived into the courtyard of the palace," said the prince. "Some enchantment from it has infected her and they must both be cured of it. When the horse is in the courtyard I will let a sweet-smelling incense free from a bottle and that will banish all the princess's ills."

The unsuspecting sultan did everything Prince Feroze asked. The prince arranged the strong, sweet-smelling incense so that it blew into the faces of the sultan and his court officials. They rubbed their eyes and lost sight of the princess and the enchanted horse. In a moment, Prince Feroze had seized the princess in his arms and mounted the enchanted horse.

He turned and called through the swirling incense: "Sultan of Kashmir, when you would marry a princess, make sure that you first obtain her consent!"

Then the prince twisted the wooden peg on the horse's back. The horse rose swiftly into the air and soon the two sweethearts were safely back in Persia.

Once again, everyone was delighted to see the prince safely home. Arrangements were made for a magnificent wedding, as befitted a great prince and a beautiful princess.

The Prince of Persia and the Princess of Bengal were married and lived for many years happily together. In due course, the prince became Sultan of Persia and was a wise and kind ruler.

As for the enchanted horse, it was shut in a secret room in the palace where it may remain to this day.

The Gnome who wanted to be King

Once upon a time there lived a gnome named Henry. He wore a red cap and a blue tunic tied round with a smart sash. He had yellow stockings and soft leather shoes.

He lived in a comfortable cottage with a thatched roof and whitewashed walls over the porchway which led into a hollow tree at the back.

It was all very cosy and quaint and *exciting* even, some folk would have thought. Some folk would have thought that living partly in a hollow tree was actually very *smart* and something to chat about with your friends.

However, Henry did not think that. He was discontented.

Henry had lived in his cottage-cum-tree-house for a very long time; several hundred years actually. Gnomes have long lives, you know, compared with humans.

"I am sick of this quiet, humble life in the country," grumbled Henry. "Up in the morning, breakfast, housework, lunch, shopping, an occasional spot of gardening, supper, have a laugh with a friend or two, hot milk and biscuits, a little reading and then bed again. It's all very well for a hundred years or so, but after the second hundred years, the excitement does begin to wear thin.

"I'm sure everyone doesn't live like this," grumbled Henry. "In fact, I know they don't."

He thought about the kings and princes in the story books he read before he went to sleep.

"*They* live in huge palaces with servants to wait on them," he thought. "*They* eat scrumptious banquets. No boiled eggs and toast fingers on a tray in front of the fire for *them. And* they wear magnificent,

fashionable clothes. You would never catch Prince Charming trotting about in a red cap and blue tunic for a hundred years on end, I am sure. Three different outfits a day for Prince Charming or the palace tailor lives on bread and water for a month and no mistake."

Henry grew more and more miserable.

Every evening he would read stories of kings and princes living colourful lives of luxury, excitement and adventure.

Every evening he would moan: "I wish I were a king. I wish I lived in a grand palace. I wish I had lots of servants. I wish I had a huge kingdom."

The birds who lived in the tree grew tired of listening to it all. They talked for hours about what could be done. Finally, they sent for a good fairy and asked her to grant Henry's wish. She was happy to oblige.

The good fairy waved her magic wand and turned Henry into a king.

Henry was absolutely amazed. One moment he was in his little cottage, wearing his red cap and blue tunic with the sash and yellow stockings and soft leather shoes. The next second he was dressed as a king, standing in a palace.

He looked round. It was all very nice.

Perhaps he should ask someone how he had got there.

Perhaps not, on second thoughts.

If people thought he was not really king, they might send him home and Henry did not want that. He liked it where he was.

A cook walked solemnly up to Henry.

"Your Majesty!" he bowed. "What would Your Majesty like for lunch?"

Henry was thrilled.

This was what he had always wanted, nice meals brought to him with no shopping, no cooking and NO WASHING UP. Not for *Henry*, anyway.

"I should like a steak and kidney pie, cream mould, cherry meringue, iced fruit and lemonade – er – please," ordered Henry, remembering just in time that kings are supposed to be noble and polite.

court officials came in, waving sheets of parchment covered with sums.

"We have not enough money to pay the army," they said. "You must think of some taxes, but the people are still grumbling about the last lot you invented. The sails you ordered for the navy ships are too long for the masts and the boots delivered for the army are all left feet and no right feet. What are you going to do about it?"

"Can't all these problems wait until I have finished my lunch?" asked Henry.

"No," replied the court officials, "we have

"Certainly, Your Majesty," smiled the cook and returned with all the food in a few moments.

Henry was thrilled and sat down to eat at once.

However, his happiness did not last. Hardly had he lifted a spoon when two

another lot of problems waiting for after lunch. These are your *before* lunch problems."

Poor Henry! He had always found it hard to eat and think at the same time.

He puzzled his brains to give the best answers he could. Then he did his best to enjoy lunch, but all the while he was dreading the questions he would have to face *after* lunch.

And so things went on. It was a life of luxury and good food and problems, problems, problems! Luckily the good fairy was nearby and she decided to intervene.

The good fairy looked at Henry, fallen asleep over his books of taxes and pages of problems.

"Would you like me to take you away from all this and make you plain Henry Gnome again?" she asked.

"Oh yes, *please!*" muttered Henry, in his sleep. "Though I don't know what you mean by *plain*. I always thought I was rather a handsome figure of a gnome and no one can say that I didn't keep myself clean and neat."

"Oh – all right. Don't go on so!" snapped the good fairy, for even good fairies can become impatient.

She waved her magic wand and Henry found himself back in his own clothes in his own cottage and he was very happy.

The Corn Fairies

Once upon a time, there was a little boy who lived in the country. He was a good-natured lad, but thoughtless.

He ran through the corn fields chasing butterflies, not thinking of the corn he was trampling, nor of the little creatures who lived amongst the corn stalks.

He did not think of the birds he startled, nor even of the butterflies, which did not much care for being chased.

"What fun it is to be running about in the fresh air!" laughed the boy. "Don't the butterflies look pretty, fluttering their wings in the sunshine! How swiftly the birds can fly! How quickly those furry little brown mice can run!"

The boy blundered and stamped wherever the fancy took him, until he grew tired and lay down to rest.

From amongst the corn stalks a corn fairy stared at him.

The corn fairy was angry. The boy had stamped on his little house and destroyed it completely.

"That boy must be taught a lesson," muttered the corn fairy. He summoned up all his magic powers and cast a spell over the sleeping boy. Gradually the lad became smaller and smaller, till at last he was no

bigger than the corn fairies themselves.

After a while, the boy awoke from his snooze in the sunny corn field. However, it did not seem to be so sunny now.

Tall, thin trees had grown up all around him and were blotting out the light. Strange, green trees with enormous, coloured flowers cast shadows on him and filled the air with heavy perfume.

"Where am I?" thought the boy. "How have I come to this strange country?"

Of course the boy was not in a strange country at all. He was exactly where he

had been before, but now he was so small that the corn looked like a forest and the flowering weeds like huge, exotic trees.

The boy heard the swish and rustle of a large person pushing towards him through the forest, as he thought the corn stalks were.

He looked up, expecting to see a fat man, perhaps a woodchopper. How amazed he was when he saw a simply enormous *hedgehog* towering over him!

"You look like that clumsy boy who was trampling over the corn field a while ago," snapped the hedgehog. "Thank goodness you have become smaller. A fine lot of

damage you were doing! Don't you ever look where you are going?"

The boy was still astonished at all he was seeing, but he had the courage to speak up for himself.

"I'm not clumsy," he replied. "And I always look where I am going, but what is there to look for out here? It doesn't matter where I tread in a corn field."

"Doesn't matter where you tread! *Doesn't matter where you tread!*" shouted the hedgehog. "You come along with me, young fellow and I will show you the damage you have done in this very corn field. You will be quite surprised!"

The boy was becoming more and more indignant. The hedgehog was a perfect stranger to him and extremely plain-looking. What right had he to take the boy to task? The boy felt he had been doing nothing wrong and yet he suddenly found himself in a strange forest with this busybody grumbling at him.

He opened his mouth to say something not at all polite, when a terrible thudding shook the ground.

THUD . . . THUD! THUD . . . THUD!

The deafening sounds came closer and closer. The ground trembled and quaked.

The boy was terrified and puzzled. He had never heard such a sound in his life before.

What could it be?

Then, with a swish and a shudder, the tall trees were swept aside and a huge pair of feet came stamping carelessly across the ground.

STOMP . . . STOMP! STOMP . . . STOMP!

The feet landed on anything and everything which lay in their path.

The boy scarcely managed to scramble aside to avoid being squashed himself.

However, even in his hurry, he could not

help noticing that the shoes and socks and trousers were exactly like those of his friend, Old George the ploughman.

The boy took a closer look at the 'forest' and the 'flowering trees'.

He began to guess what had happened to him. Then he heard the thunderous footsteps returning and tried to hide under a boulder – or a small stone – as it really was. On the other side of it he came face to face with a mouse and a corn fairy. It was the corn fairy who had bewitched him.

"How do you like being small?" the corn fairy asked the boy.

"Not much," replied the boy. "What do I have to do to get big again?"

"I can make you big again," replied the corn fairy. "It was I who made you small."

The boy glared at him.

"Thank you for nothing, then," he snapped. "Why did you pick on me?"

The corn fairy turned and pointed at his wrecked home and his face grew angry.

"Because you trod on my home and wrecked it," he said. "I wanted to show you the damage you could do by stamping carelessly through the corn field."

When the boy saw the pretty little house knocked into pieces, he did feel sorry.

"I didn't mean to do it," he said. "I didn't *know* I was doing it," he added.

And then, because he was a boy full of spirit he went on: "And actually I think it is unreasonable of you to blame me because

I cannot – could not – help being large any more than you can help being small – and when you are large it is difficult to *see* houses as small as this.

"However," went on the boy, wishing to be fair, "I will help you to rebuild your house, as I was the one responsible for knocking it down."

Several small creatures had gathered round by this time and they agreed the boy had spoken well.

"You help me rebuild the house and I will make you large again," promised the corn fairy. The boy was very relieved.

And that is exactly what happened.

"You saw how frightening it was when your friend, Old George, walked through the corn field," the corn fairy said to the boy. "Will you try to be a bit more careful where you walk in future?"

"Oh, I certainly shall," replied the boy. And indeed he was. He never forgot his corn field lesson and was careful never to tread on another fairy home ever again.

However, he did not mention this to anyone, not even Old George.

"They would never believe me," he thought. "Or else they would say it was all a dream I had while I was sleeping in the corn field in the bright, hot sun."

The Little Singing Frog

Long ago in a country called Yugoslavia, there lived a farmer and his wife who had no children. They longed to have a little baby, but their wishes were not granted.

Then one morning they found that a baby girl had been left on their doorstep. Unfortunately the child was not pretty. It had the face of a frog. Nevertheless, the kind couple took it in and brought it up as their own.

The baby grew into a strong child and had a sweet nature. The farmer and his wife loved her, but there was no denying that the poor girl was ugly and would be laughed at if she went into town.

The girl stayed at home on the farm and

seemed quite happy. She loved everything to do with nature. She helped her adopted father tend the different crops. Strangely, everything she touched grew well.

From the moment the frog girl worked on the farm the crops were twice and three times as plentiful. Not only that but the cows gave more milk, the hens laid more and bigger eggs.

The farmer and his wife often wondered if the strange child was a gift from the Earth Goddess.

"Perhaps all these good crops are a reward to us for being kind to the unfortunate little thing," said the farmer.

His wife thought he could well be right.

Another strange thing about the frog girl was that she had a beautiful voice. She would sit in the trees and sing so sweetly that the birds would answer her calls. All the fields around where she sat would be filled with the beautiful sound of her own voice and the lovely chorus of the birds singing with her.

The years went by and the girl grew up into a young woman. Still she sang in her lovely voice and still the crops grew marvellously and all the animals on the farm became fat and content. The kindly farmer in turn became quite rich.

Then, one day, a prince came riding by. He was an eager young man who felt it was his duty to ride to every part of his father's kingdom to discover what was happening and why.

He was quite surprised to find such a prosperous farm in a rather remote, poor

"Who is singing with that beautiful voice?" he asked the farmer.

Now the farmer was not at all keen to answer the prince's question.

He did not know the prince, nor whether he intended to be friendly or not. He *did* know that the frog girl was ugly and that

part of the country. It was most unusual.

The farmer was equally surprised to turn round and see a prince riding by.

As usual, the frog girl had been sitting in the tree singing. All the birds had been joining in. Amidst all the noise, the farmer had not heard the clip-clop of the prince's horse as he approached.

The prince, however, had heard all the singing and marvelled at the chorus.

the prince might laugh when he saw her, which would most surely hurt the young girl's feelings.

Country farmers in any case, are always very careful about what they say to folk from the big city, such as the prince. Folks from the big city have a nasty habit of wanting to collect taxes on all sorts of unexpected things, even girls with frog faces who sing nicely.

The farmer shrugged his shoulders and replied: "I heard only the birds singing. There was no human voice. You must have been mistaken, my lord."

The prince was not to be put off so easily. He was a very keen, observant young man who believed the evidence of his senses.

sing with other people with beautiful voices. It would be fun to give concerts."

She scrambled down the tree, ran forward to the prince and clasped his hands.

"*I* was singing," she said. "It was *my* voice you heard. I should *love* to come to

"I was not mistaken," he said. "I know a lot about singing. We have some very good singers back at the palace. They give concerts every Friday during supper. I am always looking for good singers."

By this time the frog girl was curious. She peered down at the prince. He was handsome and spoke in a firm, truthful way.

The girl thought: "I should like to go to

the palace and sing with other people, if you would let me."

The farmer looked on anxiously, thinking that the prince would be upset by the girl's frog face.

However, if the prince did think that the girl was ugly, he did not show it. He smiled at her and said he would be delighted if she would join the palace singers. The frog girl was so happy at this opportunity.

It was arranged that the frog girl should go to the palace in three weeks time and be given a room, plenty of food and should sing with the other singers.

"I shall be back from my journeys by then and I will arrange everything," said the prince. "You will be well cared for."

The farmer offered the frog girl a horse and a brand new travelling bag for her clothes. However she refused them.

"I will ride on a white cockerel and carry an ear of golden wheat in my hand," she

said. "I know that is what I should do."

When the strange-looking girl, riding a cockerel came to the palace gates, the guards laughed at her and were about to send her away, when the frog girl turned the golden wheat around in her hand.

The sun shone on the wheat and glowed on the girl. Her frog face melted away and she was transformed into the beautiful girl she was always destined to be.

As the farmer and his wife had thought, the strange baby was a gift from the Earth Goddess and had come to bring prosperity, through kindness, to the whole kingdom.

The guards stood back and let her into the palace. The prince fell in love with her as he had fallen in love with her voice. They were married and lived happily for years. Later, they became king and queen, but the girl went on singing and everywhere she went the crops grew and the land was plentiful.